Nick
and the
Canal Painter

Mary Arrigan · Debbie Boon

Go Bananas

To David and Michael with love

M.A.

For all of the little artists at
Falconer Hill Infant School

D.B.

First published in Great Britain 2004
by Egmont Books Ltd
239 Kensington High Street, London W8 6SA
Text copyright © Mary Arrigan 2004
Illustrations copyright © Debbie Boon 2004
The author and illustrator have asserted their moral rights
Paperback ISBN 1 4052 0977 1
10 9 8 7 6 5 4 3 2 1
A CIP catalogue record for this title is available from the British Library
Printed in U.A.E.

Contents

Stop teasing!

Glub, glub!

Bugface

On the Friday that he was made to wear his big, round glasses to school, Nick decided he would never speak again. His mum tried to make him talk.

'Lots of people wear glasses, honeybun,' she said. 'Superman wore glasses when he wasn't being Superman. Harry Potter wears glasses.'

His sister, Mags, tried to make Nick talk.

'You look like a fish,' she sniggered.

'Glub, glub.'

In the schoolyard things got worse.
'Nick's got goggles on!' shouted
Jason Jones. 'Bugface!'

'Yeah, Bugface,' echoed Ben
Warren, who always repeated
whatever Jason said.

Ha, ha, ha!

Before class started, Nick put his glasses
in his schoolbag. The heads of the children
in front of him were blurry,
and Miss Crane's yellow
cardie made her look like
a big canary in a fog.

'I want to tell you about an important art competition for all the junior schools in town,' Miss Crane said.

'What's the prize, Miss?' asked Jason Jones.

'Art materials,' beamed Miss Crane.

'But we'll be up against St Hilda's, Miss,' said Nellie Figgs. 'They have a posh art room.'

'I know,' sighed Miss Crane. 'And we have a few baldy brushes and hard paint.'

'We'll win, Miss,' said Becky Bee, the bossiest girl in the class, and Nick's best friend.

Nick will do a brilliant job!

'No way!' sniggered Jason Jones.

'Yeah, no way,' said Ben Warren.

Wormy Squiggles

'We'll paint a river scene,' went on Becky.
'Rivers are nice.'

'We'll do aliens zapping everyone,' said
Jason Jones. 'SPLAT! SQUELCH!'

'Yeah,' said Ben Warren. 'SQUELCH!'

'Perhaps not, Jason,' said Miss Crane.
'Everyone will paint part of the scene.
Who'll paint the river?'

'Me and Nick,' said Becky Bee proudly.

'Ha!' laughed Jason Jones. 'All Nick paints are blobs.'

Which was true. Nick's school pictures *were* just blobs compared to the ones he did in his own bedroom with his glasses on. There he loved to draw fanged monsters and mega cartoons of Jason Jones being scrunched by hairy giants.

'Cool it, Jason,' said Miss Crane.

She smiled at Nick. 'Perhaps if you, ahem, wore your glasses, Nick,' she whispered.

10

But Nick just frowned. He still wasn't talking.

'We'll draw our picture today,' said Miss Crane. 'And on Monday we'll paint it.'

Boats, thought Nick. I'll paint big, colourful boats on wavy water.

He put his face really close to the paper, but, no matter how hard he tried, the boats turned out like clumpy clogs . . .

Poor Nick.

. . . and the waves were just wormy squiggles.

'That's rotten, Nick,' said Nellie.

'Awful,' agreed the rest of the class. 'We'll never win with stuff like that.'

'Cool it, you lot,' said Becky Bee. 'They're just the rough drawings. He'll paint really brilliant boats on Monday, won't you, Nick?'

Nick sighed and wished for a colourful disease with green belly-dots and purple puke that would keep him out of school until the painting was finished.

Pongy Water

On Saturday morning, Mum flapped into Nick's room.

'Up, lazybones,' she said. 'We're going to the National Gallery. And wear your glasses.

Get used to wearing them outdoors.'

Nick groaned. I'll be bored, he thought.

Mum had a part-time job teaching Art History. She sometimes went to the big art gallery in London to write notes on the pictures there.

The pictures in the gallery reminded Nick of the art competition. He sighed heavily. Wear my glasses and the class will jeer, he thought. Don't wear my glasses and I'll mess up the picture. It's not fair.

'I'll be studying French pictures,' said Mum. 'Don't get lost, Nick.'

As soon as his mum's back was turned, Nick put his glasses into his pocket. Now all the pictures were just blurry rectangles. But one colourful painting caught his eye. He leaned closer and squinted. Sky and water and . . . were there boats?

'Keep back, kid,' muttered an attendant. 'That's a priceless Canaletto.'

I like this one!

Nick shrank back from the painting and wondered what a Canaletto was. He stared hard at the picture, wishing he could get a closer look. As he stared, the voices around him grew distant. Nick was surprised by a watery smell.

He sniffed. It smells like stinky trainers, he thought. The smell became stronger, like a river in summer. He rubbed his eyes.

This was weird.

It was time to break his silence and call out for his mum.

What's that pong?

The Canal Painter

'Mmm . . .' he began, but the word froze.
In front of him, by a big, open window, a
man was standing at an easel. The man put
down his brush and a flat thing with blobs
of paint on it, and rubbed his eyes.

17

'*Mamma mia*!' he groaned. 'These foggy eyes of mine.'

'Excuse me,' said Nick. 'Can you tell me where all the people have gone?'

The man turned around and, even without his glasses, Nick could see that he was wearing fancy dress.

'Who are you, lad?' the man asked. 'This is my studio.'

'Studio?' echoed Nick. 'This is the National Gallery and I'm here with my mum.'

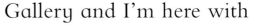

The man laughed. 'The National Whattery? What are you talking about, lad? Have you come looking for work in the studio of Antonio, the great Canaletto?'

'N . . . no,' replied Nick. 'I'm looking for my mum. I left her here somewhere.'

There were happy shouts coming from outside the window, and the splish–splash sound of boats. Nick rushed to see. He squinted very hard.

Wow! We're on a river!

'Boats?' he said. 'Are they boats, Mister?'

'Of course they're boats,' said Canaletto. 'Except that we call them gondolas. But the colours, lad.

Tell me about the colours of the costumes the people are wearing.'

Nick squinted again, but the scene remained blurred.

'Kind of runny,' he said. 'I can't really see.'

'Pah!' Canaletto said impatiently. 'What use are you, if you can't tell my tired old eyes about the colours? I have all the sketches done,' he sighed. 'But I need to have the colours just right.'

Nick put his face up close to the big canvas on the easel.

'You're painting what's out there?' he said. 'Wow!'

'Yes,' replied Canaletto. 'But so much tiny work has made my eyes tired and I can't see the little-bitty parts of the Ascension Day celebrations.

The Doge will be furious if I'm not finished on time. He has a wall ready for it to hang on in his palace.'

'What celebrations?' asked Nick. 'And who's the Doge?'

'The Doge is our ruler,' said Canaletto. 'Don't you know this is one of the great festivals of Venice? The Doge goes out in his Golden Barge to celebrate the legend of the marriage of Venice and the Sea by dropping a gold ring into the canal.'

This is the Doge.

He looks important!

'This is mad,' laughed Nick. 'Venice, huh? Get real, Mister!'

'Real?' snorted Canaletto. 'What's real, lad, is that I've given my assistants the day off, so I have no one to help me. My eyes won't work. Still so tired.' He sighed and rubbed his eyes.

And that's what gave Nick his great idea.

Lots to Do

'My glasses!' exclaimed Nick, taking them from his pocket.

'Oh, I have heard of these round glass things,' said Canaletto.

'They're great,' went on Nick. 'When you look through them, you see things more clearly. Let me show you.' He put them on and looked up at Canaletto.

Canaletto didn't laugh or call him Bugface.

'Ha, I can even see the hairs up your nose,' said Nick.

'What about the scene on the canal? Can you see that, lad?'

'Oh, wow!' Nick gasped. 'Lots of coloured boa– gondolas,' he said. 'And men in bright clothes steering with long oars. People in fancy dress are waving and shouting at the biggest gondola. It is covered in flowers and ribbons.'

'That's the Golden Barge,' said Canaletto. 'What else do you see?'

'A palace,' said Nick. 'A big, dazzling palace with loads of arches and lots of fiddly decorations.'

'The Doge's palace,' said Canaletto.

'This is wicked! I've never seen anything like it,' laughed Nick.

'You can see all that since you put those things on your face?' said Canaletto. 'Let me see.'

Nick reluctantly took off his glasses.

'*Mamma mia*!' exclaimed Canaletto as he peered through Nick's glasses. 'I can see everything! These are powerful things altogether. Come on, lad. We have lots to do.'

Squashed Beetles

Canaletto set to work at once, mixing colours on his big palette. When he added drops of oil to the colours, they became fat and glossy.

'Great colours,' said Nick, peering closely at the palette.

The names were magic to Nick – Naples Yellow, Burnt Sienna, Indigo, Ultramarine Blue.

'They are made from special clays, crushed gems and plants. That one, Crimson Lake, is made from squashed beetles,' said Canaletto, pointing to a red blob.

'Cool!' exclaimed Nick.

Nick helped by handing colours and brushes to Canaletto.

Now and then, Canaletto took off the glasses, polished them and muttered, 'Wonderful things. Wonderful.'

'Done!' he said at last. 'Another masterpiece by Antonio Canaletto.' He handed Nick the glasses. Nick studied the painting.

'Oh, wow!' he whispered. It was so realistic. 'It's all there! That's the most brilliant picture I have ever seen.'

'Thanks to your round glass things,' laughed Canaletto.

I couldn't have done it without you.

Great! Crushed beetles!

In his excitement, Nick accidentally brushed against the palette and got a smudge of Crimson Lake on his sleeve.

'Oops,' said Canaletto. 'Here, let me wipe that off.'

'No, it's OK,' said Nick. 'I'll leave it there so that I can match it to my own picture of boats.'

'Good,' said Canaletto. 'Well, with those round glass things you'll be able to see all the small details and paint as well as me, Canaletto the Canal Painter!'

'That's for sure!' laughed Nick.

Back at the Gallery

'There you are, Nick,' said Mum. 'I've been looking everywhere for you.'

Nick blinked. Where was Canaletto? Where were the laughing, colourful crowds of people in gondolas? The lapping water of the canal?

Then he saw that the scene was hanging on the wall in front of him – just as it had been on Canaletto's easel.

'Mum, you must look at this painting,' cried Nick.

'You're talking!' said Mum in surprise. 'You haven't talked for two days.'

'Of course I'm talking,' replied Nick. 'How else could I have talked to Canaletto?'

'Pardon?' said Mum.

'This painting of Ascension Day in Venice,' continued Nick. 'See? There's the Doge – he's a sort of king. He's tossed a ring into the water to celebrate the marriage of Venice and the Sea. That's his gondola.

Bless him!

I was with Canaletto when he painted it.
I lent him my glasses because his eyes were
tired and he couldn't see the little-bitty details.'

'My son the dreamer,' groaned Mum.
'And what's that big stain on your jumper?'

Nick smiled. 'Crimson Lake,'
he said. 'Did you
know that it's
made from
squashed
beetles, Mum?'

Oh, Nick!

Cheers, Canaletto!

The four junior schools were in the Town Hall putting up their pictures for judging. St Hilda's had painted a jungle with lots of hairy animals. High Street Juniors had a circus scene with clowns and skinny, upside-down people on a trapeze. Mossbank Juniors had a space scene with slimy monsters and tinfoil spaceships.

Look at theirs!

Miss Crane unrolled the Elmtree Juniors picture and, with help from her excited pupils, hung it on the wall.

Everyone stayed very quiet as the judges
made their way around the hall.
Every so often they muttered to
one another, and
made important
harrumphing
noises as they
wrote in their
notebooks.

Marvellous

We drew
that bit!

Then they came to Elmtree Junior
School's entry.

'Ooh,' said the first judge. 'Look at the
tiny people walking along the bank.
And the mad flowers and trees.

And the blazing bright sunshine and clouds . . .
and the dirty big thumbprints on the sky'
  'They did that,' the class said, pointing .to
Jason Jones and Ben Warren. 'Messy pair.'

'Well, bless my soul!' exclaimed the lady judge, her jaw dropping almost to her big, tweedy chest. 'Look at the river. Such sparkly little waves. Perfect.'

'Marvellous illustration!' said the second judge. 'Such colourful boats.'

'Gondolas, Mister,' said Becky Bee grandly. 'Nick says they're gondolas.'

'Cor! All those people waving and laughing in them. Ain't that somethin',' gasped the third judge, forgetting to speak in his posh judge voice. 'This here picture is the winner.'

And the other two judges nodded approvingly.

Nick looked at the happy faces of his cheering classmates. He could see them all clearly – Angela's freckles, Becky's new tooth, the wart on Gavin's knee, and the crinkly lines around Miss Crane's eyes.

The funny thing was, nobody had even noticed that he was wearing his glasses. Except for Jason Jones.

'Yah. Think you're great, Bugfa–'

'Get lost Jason,' said Ben Warren. 'Nick's dead brill.'

Nick looked at the red stain on his jumper which his mum hadn't succeeded in washing out.

'Cheers, Canaletto,' he said, and smiled.

Canaletto's Venice

Hello, I'm Canaletto. I was born in Venice, way back in 1697 – that's just over 300 years ago.

Venice is now a city in Italy. But in Canaletto's day, it was a country all of its own, ruled by a man called the Doge.

The Venice of today looks almost exactly the same as when Canaletto lived there – isn't that amazing?

But what makes Venice so very special, is that it's a whole city built on several islands in the sea. This means that all its roads and streets are canals. To get about, people who live in Venice use boats – there are no cars or lorries. There's even a riverboat bus!

Wow! Imagine taking a boat to school every day!

Canaletto was a **view painter**. A view is a real scene or landscape. Venice is a very special city to paint. There are no hills, so the skies seem huge! With so much water around there are always rippling reflections.

I was the *best view* painter of my time!

Telling stories with pictures

As we know from the story, Canaletto's big painting illustrates a scene from the wonderful story of the Doge and his golden ring.

Gondolas are the taxis of Venice!

The Doge's palace – the biggest and grandest in Venice!

The Doge's golden barge.

You can still hitch a ride in a gondola today!

Canaletto chose to paint the scene where the Doge returns to Venice after throwing his special ring into the sea. Do you think this is the most exciting part of the story? Which bit would **you** choose to illustrate?

I wanted to show my wonderful Venice, and all the people celebrating!

I would have painted the Doge throwing the ring into the water!

You too can be a view painter!

You will need:

1 piece A4 coloured card – choose your favourite colour!
1 piece A4 drawing paper
1 pair scissors
Sticky tape
Coloured pencils, pens, paint or crayons
– whatever you have.
1 grown-up to help cut the card

First, make your special frame. Take the A4 card, fold it in half and ask a grown-up to help you cut a square out of the middle, like this:

Now open it up, and **ta-da**!
You have your special frame!

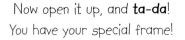

portrait

landscape

Choose a closed window in your house or flat, hold the frame up before your eyes, and look through it, out of the window. Choose a view that interests you. It could be of a garden, it could be of a countryside scene, a street, other houses, or rooftops!

Turn the frame around for portrait or landscape.

When you are happy with your view, stick your frame on to the window with sticky tape. (Better check with a grown-up that it's OK to do this.)

Now choose your **materials**. Canaletto used oil paints for his paintings. Debbie Boon, the illustrator of this book, uses acrylic paint. What materials do **you** have for colouring in? Paint, crayons, pencils, felt-tips?

Debbie Boon

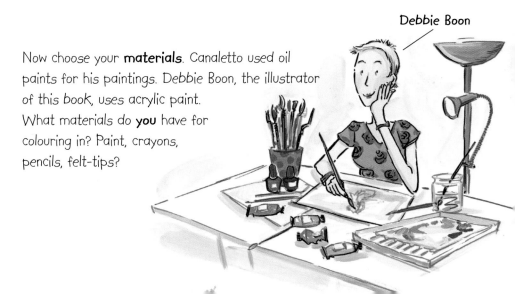

Now sit down in front of the window, and draw or paint the scene you have chosen on the piece of blank A4 drawing paper.

When you've finished your picture, carefully take your frame off the window. Using glue, stick the frame on to the picture, and lo and behold, your very own masterpiece!